DANIEL TIGER'S NEIGHBORHOOD®

Who Can? Daniel Can!

By Maggie Testa
Poses and layouts by Jason Fruchter

Ready-to-Read

SIMON SPOTLIGHT

An imprint of Simon & Schuster Children's Publishing Division New York London Toronto Sydney New Delhi 1230 Avenue of the Americas, New York, New York 10020   This Simon Spotlight edition May 2017 © 2017 The Fred Rogers Company. All rights reserved, including the right of reproduction in whole or in part in any form. SIMON SPOTLIGHT, READY-TO-READ, and colophon are registered trademarks of Simon & Schuster, Inc. For information about special discounts for bulk purchases, please contact Simon & Schuster Special Sales at 1-866-506-1949 or business@simonandschuster.com. Manufactured in the United States of America 0317 LAK 2 4 6 8 10 9 7 5 3 1 ISBN 978-1-4814-9519-6 (hc) ISBN 978-1-4814-9518-9 (pbk) ISBN 978-1-4814-9520-2 (eBook)

Here is a list of all the words you will find in this book. Sound them out before you begin reading the story.

Names:

Daniel Tiger

Katerina

Miss Elaina

O

Prince Wednesday

Word families:

"-ame"	→	game	name
"-and"	→	land	sand
"-ug"	→	bug	hug
"-ump"	→	bump	jump

Sight words:

a	and	are	ball	can
dance	do	give	how	I
in	is	make	my	our
play	show	the	us	we
what	you			

Bonus words:

friends	Hello	Good-bye

Ready to go? Happy reading!

Don't miss the questions about the story
on the last page of this book.

Hello! My name is
Daniel Tiger.

We can play a game.

What can
our friends do?

Hello, Katerina!
How are you?

Show us
what you can do.

Katerina can
dance in the sand!

Hello, O!
How are you?

Show us
what you can do.

O can jump and land!

Hello,
Prince Wednesday!
How are you?

Show us
what you can do.

Prince Wednesday can bump the ball!

Hello, Miss Elaina!
How are you?

Show us
what you can do.

Miss Elaina
can make a bug.

What can I do?

I can give a hug.

What can you do?

Good-bye!

Now that you have read the story, can you answer these questions?

1. Where does this story take place?

2. Can you do some of the things in this story? Which ones?

3. In this story, you read the words "land" and "sand." Those words rhyme. Can you think of other words that rhyme with "land" and "sand"?

Great job!
You are a reading star!